NOW YOU CAN READ....

Rumpelstiltskin

STORY ADAPTED BY LUCY KINCAID

ILLUSTRATED BY ERIC KINCAID

© 1983 The Rourke Corporation, Inc.

Published by The Rourke Corporation, Inc., P.O. Box 711, Windermere, Florida 32786. Copyright © 1983 by The Rourke Corporation, Inc. All copyrights reserved. No part of this book may be reproduced in any form without written permission from the publisher. Printed in the United States of America.

Library of Congress Cataloging in Publication Data

Kincaid, Lucy.
  Rumpelstiltskin.

  (Now you can read)
  Reprint. Originally published: Cambridge [Cambridgeshire]: Brimax Books, © 1980.
  Summary: When a little man reappears to claim the first-born child promised him by the Queen in exchange for his help in spinning straw to gold, he gives her a chance to keep the child if she guesses his name.
  [1. Fairy tales. 2. Folklore—Germany] I. Rowe, Eric, 1938- ill. 2. Rumpelstiltskin (Folk tale). English. III. Title. IV. Series: Kincaid, Lucy, Now you can read.
  PZ8.K53Ru 1983   398.2'1'0943   [E]   82-21589
  ISBN 0-86592-177-6

THE ROURKE CORPORATION, INC.
Windermere, Florida 32786

NOW YOU CAN READ....

Rumpelstiltskin

Once there was a miller who had a beautiful daughter. He was always bragging about her. Sometimes he said things that were not true. One day he said, "My daughter is so clever she can spin straw into gold."

The King heard about the miller's
daughter and sent for her.
"You shall spin straw into gold
for ME!" he said.
The miller's daughter wanted to say
that she could not. But, she had
never seen a king before and she
was afraid to speak.

The King took her to a room where there was a spinning wheel and a pile of straw.

"If you value your life," he said sternly, "you will spin all that straw into gold by morning."

With that, he left the room and locked the door behind him.

The miller's daughter began to cry.
She did not know WHAT to do.
Then, through her tears, she saw a
tiny man with a long white beard. He
was standing beside the spinning wheel.
"What will you
give me if I spin
the straw into
gold for you?" he
asked.
"I will give you
my necklace," she
said, quickly
drying her tears.

The next morning the King
unlocked the door. The straw was
gone. In its place was a heap
of gold. The miller's daughter
was sorting the golden coins into
piles.

That night the King led her back to the same room. This time the straw stretched from wall to wall. It reached as high as the window. "If you value your life," said the King sternly, "spin all THAT into gold by morning."

As soon as the door was locked the little man appeared. "What will you give me if I help you this time?" he asked. "My ring," replied the miller's daughter. She took the ring from her finger.

When the King saw the huge pile of gold next morning he was very pleased. He led the miller's daughter to another room. There the straw was piled so high it touched the ceiling.

"Spin all THAT into gold and you shall be my Queen," he said.

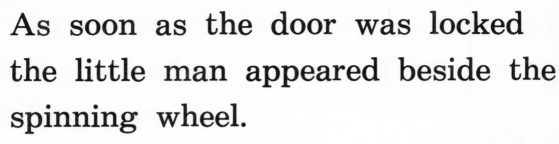

As soon as the door was locked the little man appeared beside the spinning wheel.

"I have nothing left to give you," said the miller's daughter sadly.

"Give me the first child born to you when you are Queen," said the little man.

The miller's daughter wanted to be Queen, so she agreed. The little man began to spin.

A few days later the miller's daughter married the King, and became Queen. What a lot of boasting her father did THAT day!

A whole year went by and the new Queen forgot about the little man. Then, one day, there was great excitement at the palace. A baby had been born.

The excitement quickly changed to weeping and crying when the little man appeared.

"I will give you all the treasure in the kingdom. Please let me keep my baby," wept the Queen.

"You made a promise. You must keep it," said the little man. The Queen held the baby so tightly that at last he said to her, "You may keep the child if you can tell me my name within the next three days ."

The Queen lay awake, thinking, all night. "Is your name Grizzlebeard?" she asked, next morning.

"No!"

"Is it Firkin?"

"It is not!"

"Is it Bodkin?"

"No!"

On the second day, after another sleepless night, the Queen asked,

"Is your name Shortlegs?"

"No!"

"Is it Longears?"

"No!"

"Is it Pipkin?"

"No!"

The Queen just HAD to get the name right. She sent her servants far and wide across the land in search of names that were strange or different. One of the grooms was riding through a wood when he heard someone singing.
He stopped his horse and got off.

He crept closer and saw a little
man dancing around a fire.
He was singing to himself,
　　"Today I bake, tomorrow brew.
　　What a clever thing I do.
　　Soon a baby I will claim.
　　Rumpelstiltskin is my name."

The servant rode back to the palace as fast as he could. He told the Queen all that he had seen and heard.

The next day the little man
appeared at the palace. The Queen
asked, "Is your name Harry?"
"No!"
"Is it Timothy?"
"No!"
"Could it be ... Rumpelstiltskin?"

"A witch must have told you THAT!"
shouted the little man in a rage.
He was so angry he stamped his
feet. One foot went right
through the floor. He had
to pull it out with his hands.

He had made a promise. He had
to keep it. The baby was safe.

All these appear in the pages of the story. Can you find them.

miller's daughter

King

spinning wheel

straw

little man

necklace

baby

ring

Use the pictures to tell the story
in your own words. Then, draw
your own pictures.